OEDIPUS REX

By Sophocles

ARGUMENT

To Laius, King of Thebes, an oracle foretold that the child born to him by his queen Jocasta would slay his father and wed his mother. So when in time a son was born the infant's feet were riveted together and he was left to die on Mount Cithaeron. But a shepherd found the babe and tended him, and delivered him to another shepherd who took him to his master, the King or Corinth. Polybus being childless adopted the boy, who grew up believing that he was indeed the King's son. Afterwards doubting his parentage he inquired of the Delphic god and heard himself the weird declared before to Laius. Wherefore he fled from what he deemed his father's house and in his flight he encountered and unwillingly slew his father Laius. Arriving at Thebes he answered the riddle of the Sphinx and the grateful Thebans made their deliverer king. So he reigned in the room of Laius, and espoused the widowed queen. Children were born to them and Thebes prospered under his rule, but again a grievous plague fell upon the city. Again the oracle was consulted and it bade them purge themselves of blood-guiltiness. Oedipus denounces the crime of which he is unaware, and undertakes to track out the criminal. Step by step it is brought home to him that he is the man. The closing scene reveals Jocasta slain by her own hand and Oedipus blinded by his own act and praying for death or exile.

DRAMATIS PERSONAE

Oedipus
The Priest of Zeus
Creon
Chorus of Theban Elders
Teiresias
Jocasta
Messenger
Herd of Laius
Second Messenger

OEDIPUS THE KING

Scene: Thebes. Before the Palace of Oedipus.

Suppliants of all ages are seated round the altar at the palace doors, at their head a PRIEST OF ZEUS. To them enter OEDIPUS.

OEDIPUS
My children, latest born to Cadmus old,

Why sit ye here as suppliants, in your hands

Branches of olive filleted with wool?

What means this reek of incense everywhere,

And everywhere laments and litanies?

Children, it were not meet that I should learn

From others, and am hither come, myself,

I Oedipus, your world-renowned king.

Ho! aged sire, whose venerable locks

Proclaim thee spokesman of this company,

Explain your mood and purport. Is it dread

Of ill that moves you or a boon ye crave?

My zeal in your behalf ye cannot doubt;

Ruthless indeed were I and obdurate

If such petitioners as you I spurned.

PRIEST

Yea, Oedipus, my sovereign lord and king,

Thou seest how both extremes of age besiege

Thy palace altars--fledglings hardly winged, and greybeards bowed with years; priests, as am I of

Zeus, and these the flower of our youth.

Meanwhile, the common folk, with wreathed boughs

Crowd our two market-places, or before

Both shrines of Pallas congregate, or where

Ismenus gives his oracles by fire.

For, as thou seest thyself, our ship of State,

Sore buffeted, can no more lift her head,

Foundered beneath a weltering surge of blood.

A blight is on our harvest in the ear,

A blight upon the grazing flocks and herds,

A blight on wives in travail; and withal

Armed with his blazing torch the God of Plague

Hath swooped upon our city emptying

The house of Cadmus, and the murky realm

Of Pluto is full fed with groans and tears.

Therefore, O King, here at thy hearth we sit,

I and these children; not as deeming thee

A new divinity, but the first of men;

First in the common accidents of life,

And first in visitations of the Gods.

Art thou not he who coming to the town of

Cadmus freed us from the tax we paid

To the fell songstress? Nor hadst thou received

Prompting from us or been by others schooled;

No, by a god inspired (so all men deem,

And testify) didst thou renew our life.

And now, O Oedipus, our peerless king,

All we thy votaries beseech thee, find

Some succor, whether by a voice from heaven

Whispered, or haply known by human wit.

Tried counselors, methinks, are aptest found

To furnish for the future pregnant rede.

Upraise, O chief of men, upraise our State!

Look to thy laurels! for thy zeal of yore

Our country's savior thou art justly hailed:

O never may we thus record thy reign:--

"He raised us up only to cast us down."

Uplift us, build our city on a rock.

Thy happy star ascendant brought us luck,

O let it not decline! If thou wouldst rule

This land, as now thou reignest, better sure

To rule a peopled than a desert realm.

Nor battlements nor galleys aught avail,

If men to man and guards to guard them tail.

OEDIPUS
Ah! my poor children, known, ah, known too well,

The quest that brings you hither and your need.

Ye sicken all, well wot I, yet my pain,

How great soever yours, out-tops it all.

Your sorrow touches each man severally,

Him and none other, but I grieve at once

Both for the general and myself and you.

Therefore ye rouse no sluggard from day-dreams.

Many, my children, are the tears I've wept,

And threaded many a maze of weary thought.

Thus pondering one clue of hope I caught,

And tracked it up; I have sent Menoeceus' son,

Creon, my consort's brother, to inquire

Of Pythian Phoebus at his Delphic shrine,

How I might save the State by act or word.

And now I reckon up the tale of days

Since he set forth, and marvel how he fares.

'Tis strange, this endless tarrying, passing strange.

But when he comes, then I were base indeed,

If I perform not all the god declares.

PRIEST
Thy words are well timed; even as thou speakest

That shouting tells me Creon is at hand.

OEDIPUS
O King Apollo! may his joyous looks

Be presage of the joyous news he brings!

PRIEST
As I surmise, 'tis welcome; else his head

Had scarce been crowned with berry-laden bays.

OEDIPUS
We soon shall know; he's now in earshot range. *[Enter CREON]*

My royal cousin, say, Menoeceus' child,

What message hast thou brought us from the god?

CREON
Good news, for e'en intolerable ills,

Finding right issue, tend to naught but good.

OEDIPUS
How runs the oracle? thus far thy words

Give me no ground for confidence or fear.

CREON
If thou wouldst hear my message publicly,

I'll tell thee straight, or with thee pass within.

OEDIPUS
Speak before all; the burden that I bear

Is more for these my subjects than myself.

CREON
Let me report then all the god declared.

King Phoebus bids us straitly extirpate

A fell pollution that infests the land,

And no more harbor an inveterate sore.

OEDIPUS
What expiation means he? What's amiss?

* * *

CREON

Banishment, or the shedding blood for blood.

This stain of blood makes shipwreck of our state.

OEDIPUS

Whom can he mean, the miscreant thus denounced?

CREON

Before thou didst assume the helm of State,

The sovereign of this land was Laius.

OEDIPUS

I heard as much, but never saw the man.

CREON

He fell; and now the god's command is plain:

Punish his takers-off, whoe'er they be.

OEDIPUS

Where are they? Where in the wide world to find

The far, faint traces of a bygone crime?

CREON

In this land, said the god; "who seeks shall find;

Who sits with folded hands or sleeps is blind."

OEDIPUS

Was he within his palace, or afield,

Or traveling, when Laius met his fate?

* * *

CREON

Abroad; he started, so he told us, bound

For Delphi, but he never thence returned.

OEDIPUS

Came there no news, no fellow-traveler

To give some clue that might be followed up?

CREON

But one escape, who flying for dear life,

Could tell of all he saw but one thing sure.

OEDIPUS

And what was that? One clue might lead us far,

With but a spark of hope to guide our quest.

CREON

Robbers, he told us, not one bandit but

A troop of knaves, attacked and murdered him.

OEDIPUS

Did any bandit dare so bold a stroke,

Unless indeed he were suborned from Thebes?

CREON

So 'twas surmised, but none was found to avenge

His murder mid the trouble that ensued.

* * *

OEDIPUS

What trouble can have hindered a full quest,

When royalty had fallen thus miserably?

CREON

The riddling Sphinx compelled us to let slide

The dim past and attend to instant needs.

OEDIPUS

Well, I will start afresh and once again

Make dark things clear. Right worthy the concern

Of Phoebus, worthy thine too, for the dead;

I also, as is meet, will lend my aid

To avenge this wrong to Thebes and to the god.

Not for some far-off kinsman, but myself,

Shall I expel this poison in the blood;

For whoso slew that king might have a mind

To strike me too with his assassin hand.

Therefore in righting him I serve myself.

Up, children, haste ye, quit these altar stairs,

Take hence your suppliant wands, go summon hither

The Theban commons. With the god's good help

Success is sure; 'tis ruin if we fail.

[Exeunt OEDIPUS and CREON]

PRIEST

Come, children, let us hence; these gracious words

Forestall the very purpose of our suit.

And may the god who sent this oracle

Save us withal and rid us of this pest.

[Exeunt PRIEST and SUPPLIANTS]

CHORUS

(Str. 1)

Sweet-voiced daughter of Zeus from thy gold-paved Pythian shrine

Wafted to Thebes divine,

What dost thou bring me?

My soul is racked and shivers with fear.

(Healer of Delos, hear!)

Hast thou some pain unknown before,

Or with the circling years renewest a penance of yore?

Offspring of golden Hope, thou voice immortal, O tell me.

(Ant. 1)
First on Athene I call; O Zeus-born goddess, defend!

Goddess and sister, befriend,

Artemis, Lady of Thebes, high-throned in the midst of our mart!

Lord of the death-winged dart!

Your threefold aid I crave

From death and ruin our city to save.

If in the days of old when we nigh had perished, ye drave

From our land the fiery plague,

be near us now and defend us!

(Str. 2)
Ah me, what countless woes are mine!

All our host is in decline;

Weaponless my spirit lies.

Earth her gracious fruits denies;

Women wail in barren throes;

Life on life downstriken goes,

Swifter than the wind bird's flight,

Swifter than the Fire-God's might,

To the westering shores of Night.

(Ant. 2)
Wasted thus by death on death

All our city perisheth.

Corpses spread infection round;

None to tend or mourn is found.

Wailing on the altar stair

Wives and grandams rend the air--

Long-drawn moans and piercing cries

Blent with prayers and litanies.

Golden child of Zeus, O hear

Let thine angel face appear!

(Str. 3)
And grant that Ares whose hot breath I feel,

Though without targe or steel

He stalks, whose voice is as the battle shout,

May turn in sudden rout,

To the unharbored Thracian waters sped,

Or Amphitrite's bed.

For what night leaves undone,

Smit by the morrow's sun

Perisheth. Father Zeus, whose hand

Doth wield the lightning brand,

Slay him beneath thy levin bold, we pray,

Slay him, O slay!

(Ant. 3)
O that thine arrows too, Lycean King,

From that taut bow's gold string,

Might fly abroad, the champions of our rights;

Yea, and the flashing lights

Of Artemis, wherewith the huntress sweeps

Across the Lycian steeps.

Thee too I call with golden-snooded hair,

Whose name our land doth bear,

Bacchus to whom thy Maenads Evoe shout;

Come

with thy bright torch, rout,

Blithe god whom we adore,

The god whom gods abhor.

[Enter OEDIPUS.]

OEDIPUS

Ye pray; 'tis well, but would ye hear my words

And heed them and apply the remedy,

Ye might perchance find comfort and relief.

Mind you, I speak as one who comes a stranger

To this report, no less than to the crime;

For how unaided could I track it far

Without a clue? Which lacking (for too late

Was I enrolled a citizen of Thebes)

This proclamation I address to all:--

Thebans, if any knows the man by whom

Laius, son of Labdacus, was slain,

I summon him to make clean shrift to me.

And if he shrinks, let him reflect that thus

Confessing he shall 'scape the capital charge;

For the worst penalty that shall befall him

Is banishment--unscathed he shall depart.

But if an alien from a foreign land

Be known to any as the murderer,

Let him who knows speak out, and he shall have

Due recompense from me and thanks to boot.

But if ye still keep silence, if through fear

For self or friends ye disregard my hest,

Hear what I then resolve; I lay my ban

On the assassin whosoe'er he be.

Let no man in this land, whereof I hold

The sovereign rule, harbor or speak to him;

Give him no part in prayer or sacrifice

Or lustral rites, but hound him from your homes.

For this is our defilement, so the god

Hath lately shown to me by oracles.

Thus as their champion I maintain the cause

Both of the god and of the murdered King.

And on the murderer this curse I lay

(On him and all the partners in his guilt):--

Wretch, may he pine in utter wretchedness!

And for myself, if with my privity

He gain admittance to my hearth, I pray

The curse I laid on others fall on me.

See that ye give effect to all my hest,

For my sake and the god's and for our land,

A desert blasted by the wrath of heaven.

For, let alone the god's express command,

It were a scandal ye should leave unpurged

The murder of a great man and your king,

Nor track it home. And now that I am lord,

Successor to his throne, his bed, his wife,

(And had he not been frustrate in the hope

Of issue, common children of one womb

Had forced a closer bond twixt him and me,

But Fate swooped down upon him), therefore I

His blood-avenger will maintain his cause

As though he were my sire, and leave no stone

Unturned to track the assassin or avenge

The son of Labdacus, of Polydore,

Of Cadmus, and Agenor first of the race.

And for the disobedient thus I pray:

May the gods send them neither timely fruits

Of earth, nor teeming increase of the womb,

But may they waste and pine, as now they waste,

Aye and worse stricken; but to all of you,

My loyal subjects who approve my acts,

May Justice, our ally, and all the gods

Be gracious and attend you evermore.

CHORUS
The oath thou profferest, sire, I take and swear.

I slew him not myself, nor can I name

The slayer. For the quest, 'twere well, methinks

That Phoebus, who proposed the riddle, himself

Should give the answer--who the murderer was.

OEDIPUS
Well argued; but no living man can hope

To force the gods to speak against their will.

CHORUS
May I then say what seems next best to me?

* * *

OEDIPUS

Aye, if there be a third best, tell it too.

CHORUS

My liege, if any man sees eye to eye

With our lord Phoebus, 'tis our prophet, lord Teiresias;

he of all men best might guide

A searcher of this matter to the light.

OEDIPUS

Here too my zeal has nothing lagged, for twice

At Creon's instance have I sent to fetch him,

And long I marvel why he is not here.

CHORUS

I mind me too of rumors long ago--

Mere gossip.

OEDIPUS

Tell them, I would fain know all.

CHORUS

'Twas said he fell by travelers.

OEDIPUS

So I heard,

But none has seen the man who saw him fall.

* * *

CHORUS
Well, if he knows what fear is, he will quail

And flee before the terror of thy curse.

OEDIPUS
Words scare not him who blenches not at deeds.

CHORUS
But here is one to arraign him. Lo, at length

They bring the god-inspired seer in whom

Above all other men is truth inborn.

[Enter TEIRESIAS, led by a boy.]

OEDIPUS
Teiresias, seer who comprehendest all,

Lore of the wise and hidden mysteries,

High things of heaven and low things of the earth,

Thou knowest, though thy blinded eyes see naught,

What plague infects our city; and we turn

To thee, O seer, our one defense and shield.

The purport of the answer that the God

Returned to us who sought his oracle,

The messengers have doubtless told thee--how

One course alone could rid us of the pest,

To find the murderers of Laius,

And slay them or expel them from the land.

Therefore begrudging neither augury

Nor other divination that is thine,

O save thyself, thy country, and thy king,

Save all from this defilement of blood shed.

On thee we rest. This is man's highest end,

To others' service all his powers to lend.

TEIRESIAS
Alas, alas, what misery to be wise

When wisdom profits nothing!

This old lore I had forgotten; else I were not here.

OEDIPUS
What ails thee? Why this melancholy mood?

TEIRESIAS
Let me go home; prevent me not; 'twere best

That thou shouldst bear thy burden and I mine.

* * *

OEDIPUS

For shame! no true-born Theban patriot

Would thus withhold the word of prophecy.

TEIRESIAS

Thy words, O king, are wide of the mark, and I

For fear lest I too trip like thee...

OEDIPUS

Oh speak,

Withhold not, I adjure thee, if thou know'st,

Thy knowledge. We are all thy suppliants.

TEIRESIAS

Aye, for ye all are witless, but my voice

Will ne'er reveal my miseries--or thine.

OEDIPUS

What then, thou knowest, and yet willst not speak!

Wouldst thou betray us and destroy the State?

TEIRESIAS

I will not vex myself nor thee. Why ask

Thus idly what from me thou shalt not learn?

OEDIPUS

Monster! thy silence would incense a flint.

Will nothing loose thy tongue?

Can nothing melt thee,

Or shake thy dogged taciturnity?

TEIRESIAS

Thou blam'st my mood and seest not thine own

Wherewith thou art mated; no, thou taxest me.

OEDIPUS

And who could stay his choler when he heard

How insolently thou dost flout the State?

TEIRESIAS

Well, it will come what will, though I be mute.

OEDIPUS

Since come it must, thy duty is to tell me.

TEIRESIAS

I have no more to say; storm as thou willst,

And give the rein to all thy pent-up rage.

OEDIPUS

Yea, I am wroth, and will not stint my words,

But speak my whole mind. Thou methinks thou art he,

Who planned the crime, aye, and performed it too,

All save the assassination; and if thou

Hadst not been blind, I had been sworn to boot

That thou alone didst do the bloody deed.

TEIRESIAS

Is it so? Then I charge thee to abide

By thine own proclamation; from this day

Speak not to these or me.

Thou art the man,

Thou the accursed polluter of this land.

OEDIPUS

Vile slanderer, thou blurtest forth these taunts,

And think'st forsooth as seer to go scot free.

TEIRESIAS

Yea, I am free, strong in the strength of truth.

OEDIPUS

Who was thy teacher? not methinks thy art.

TEIRESIAS

Thou, goading me against my will to speak.

OEDIPUS

What speech? repeat it and resolve my doubt.

TEIRESIAS

Didst miss my sense wouldst thou goad me on?

OEDIPUS

I but half caught thy meaning; say it again.

* * *

TEIRESIAS

I say thou art the murderer of the man

Whose murderer thou pursuest.

OEDIPUS

Thou shalt rue it

Twice to repeat so gross a calumny.

TEIRESIAS

Must I say more to aggravate thy rage?

OEDIPUS

Say all thou wilt; it will be but waste of breath.

TEIRESIAS

I say thou livest with thy nearest kin

In infamy, unwitting in thy shame.

OEDIPUS

Think'st thou for aye unscathed to wag thy tongue?

TEIRESIAS

Yea, if the might of truth can aught prevail.

OEDIPUS

With other men, but not with thee, for thou

In ear, wit, eye, in everything art blind.

TEIRESIAS

Poor fool to utter gibes at me which all

Here present will cast back on thee ere long.

OEDIPUS
Offspring of endless

Night, thou hast no power

O'er me or any man who sees the sun.

TEIRESIAS
No, for thy weird is not to fall by me.

I leave to Apollo what concerns the god.

OEDIPUS
Is this a plot of Creon, or thine own?

TEIRESIAS
Not Creon, thou thyself art thine own bane.

OEDIPUS
O wealth and empiry and skill by skill

Outwitted in the battlefield of life,

What spite and envy follow in your train!

See, for this crown the State conferred on me.

A gift, a thing I sought not, for this crown

The trusty Creon, my familiar friend,

Hath lain in wait to oust me and suborned

This mountebank, this juggling charlatan,

This tricksy beggar-priest, for gain alone

Keen-eyed, but in his proper art stone-blind.

Say, sirrah, hast thou ever proved thyself

A prophet? When the riddling Sphinx was here

Why hadst thou no deliverance for this folk?

And yet the riddle was not to be solved

By guess-work but required the prophet's art;

Wherein thou wast found lacking; neither birds

Nor sign from heaven helped thee, but I came,

The simple Oedipus; I stopped her mouth

By mother wit, untaught of auguries.

This is the man whom thou wouldst undermine,

In hope to reign with Creon in my stead.

Methinks that thou and thine abettor soon

Will rue your plot to drive the scapegoat out.

Thank thy grey hairs that thou hast still to learn

What chastisement such arrogance deserves.

CHORUS
To us it seems that both the seer and thou,

O Oedipus, have spoken angry words.

This is no time to wrangle but consult

How best we may fulfill the oracle.

TEIRESIAS

King as thou art, free speech at least is mine

To make reply; in this I am thy peer.

I own no lord but Loxias; him I serve

And ne'er can stand enrolled as Creon's man.

Thus then I answer: since thou hast not spared

To twit me with my blindness--thou hast eyes,

Yet see'st not in what misery thou art fallen,

Nor where thou dwellest nor with whom for mate.

Dost know thy lineage? Nay, thou know'st it not,

And all unwitting art a double foe

To thine own kin, the living and the dead;

Aye and the dogging curse of mother and sire

One day shall drive thee, like a two-edged sword,

Beyond our borders, and the eyes that now

See clear shall henceforward endless night.

Ah whither shall thy bitter cry not reach,

What crag in all Cithaeron but shall then

Reverberate thy wail, when thou hast found

With what a hymeneal thou wast borne

Home, but to no fair haven, on the gale!

Aye, and a flood of ills thou guessest not

Shall set thyself and children in one line.

Flout then both Creon and my words, for none

Of mortals shall be stricken worse than thou.

OEDIPUS
Must I endure this fellow's insolence?

A murrain on thee! Get thee hence!

Begone Avaunt! and never cross my threshold more.

TEIRESIAS
I ne'er had come hadst thou not bidden me.

OEDIPUS
I know not thou wouldst utter folly, else

Long hadst thou waited to be summoned here.

TEIRESIAS
Such am I--as it seems to thee a fool,

But to the parents who begat thee, wise.

OEDIPUS
What sayest thou--"parents"?

Who begat me, speak?

* * *

TEIRESIAS
This day shall be thy birth-day, and thy grave.

OEDIPUS
Thou lov'st to speak in riddles and dark words.

TEIRESIAS
In reading riddles who so skilled as thou?

OEDIPUS
Twit me with that wherein my greatness lies.

TEIRESIAS
And yet this very greatness proved thy bane.

OEDIPUS
No matter if I saved the commonwealth.

TEIRESIAS
'Tis time I left thee. Come, boy, take me home.

OEDIPUS
Aye, take him quickly, for his presence irks

And lets me; gone, thou canst not plague me more.

TEIRESIAS
I go, but first will tell thee why I came.

Thy frown I dread not, for thou canst not harm me.

Hear then: this man whom thou hast sought to arrest

With threats and warrants this long while, the wretch

31

Who murdered Laius--that man is here.

He passes for an alien in the land

But soon shall prove a Theban, native born.

And yet his fortune brings him little joy;

For blind of seeing, clad in beggar's weeds,

For purple robes, and leaning on his staff,

To a strange land he soon shall grope his way.

And of the children, inmates of his home,

He shall be proved the brother and the sire,

Of her who bare him son and husband both,

Co-partner, and assassin of his sire.

Go in and ponder this, and if thou find

That I have missed the mark, henceforth declare

I have no wit nor skill in prophecy.

[Exeunt TEIRESIAS and OEDIPUS]

CHORUS
(Str. 1)
Who is he by voice immortal named from Pythia's rocky cell,

Doer of foul deeds of bloodshed, horrors that no tongue can tell?

A foot for flight he needs

Fleeter than storm-swift steeds,

For on his heels doth follow,

Armed with the lightnings of his Sire, Apollo.

Like sleuth-hounds too

The Fates pursue.

(Ant. 1)
Yea, but now flashed forth the summons from Parnassus' snowy peak,

"Near and far the undiscovered doer of this murder seek!"

Now like a sullen bull he roves

Through forest brakes and upland groves,

And vainly seeks to fly

The doom that ever nigh

Flits o'er his head,

Still by the avenging Phoebus sped,

The voice divine,

From Earth's mid shrine.

(Str. 2)

Sore perplexed am I by the words of the master seer.

Are they true, are they false? I know not and bridle my tongue for

fear, Fluttered with vague surmise;

nor present nor future is clear.

Quarrel of ancient date or in days still near know I none

Twixt the Labdacidan house and our ruler, Polybus' son.

Proof is there none: how then can I challenge our King's good name,

How in a blood-feud join for an untracked deed of shame?

(Ant. 2)
All wise are Zeus and Apollo, and nothing is hid from their ken;

They are gods; and in wits a man may surpass his fellow men;

But that a mortal seer knows more than I know--where

Hath this been proven? Or how without sign assured, can I blame

Him who saved our State when the winged songstress came,

Tested and tried in the light of us all, like gold assayed?

How can I now assent when a crime is on Oedipus laid?

CREON
Friends, countrymen, I learn King Oedipus

Hath laid against me a most grievous charge,

And come to you protesting. If he deems

That I have harmed or injured him in aught

By word or deed in this our present trouble,

I care not to prolong the span of life,

Thus ill-reputed; for the calumny

Hits not a single blot, but blasts my name,

If by the general voice I am denounced

False to the State and false by you my friends.

CHORUS
This taunt, it well may be, was blurted out

In petulance, not spoken advisedly.

CREON
Did any dare pretend that it was I

Prompted the seer to utter a forged charge?

CHORUS
Such things were said; with what intent I know not.

CREON
Were not his wits and vision all astray

When upon me he fixed this monstrous charge?

CHORUS
I know not; to my sovereign's acts I am blind.

But lo, he comes to answer for himself.

* * *

[Enter OEDIPUS.]

OEDIPUS

Sirrah, what mak'st thou here? Dost thou presume

To approach my doors, thou brazen-faced rogue,

My murderer and the filcher of my crown?

Come, answer this, didst thou detect in me

Some touch of cowardice or witlessness,

That made thee undertake this enterprise?

I seemed forsooth too simple to perceive

The serpent stealing on me in the dark,

Or else too weak to scotch it when I saw.

This thou art witless seeking to possess

Without a following or friends the crown,

A prize that followers and wealth must win.

CREON

Attend me. Thou hast spoken, 'tis my turn

To make reply. Then having heard me, judge.

OEDIPUS

Thou art glib of tongue, but I am slow to learn

Of thee; I know too well thy venomous hate.

CREON

First I would argue out this very point.

OEDIPUS

O argue not that thou art not a rogue.

CREON

If thou dost count a virtue stubbornness,

Unschooled by reason, thou art much astray.

OEDIPUS

If thou dost hold a kinsman may be wronged,

And no pains follow, thou art much to seek.

CREON

Therein thou judgest rightly, but this wrong

That thou allegest--tell me what it is.

OEDIPUS

Didst thou or didst thou not advise that I

Should call the priest?

CREON

Yes, and I stand to it.

OEDIPUS

Tell me how long is it since Laius...

CREON

Since Laius...? I follow not thy drift.

OEDIPUS

By violent hands was spirited away.

CREON

In the dim past, a many years agone.

OEDIPUS

Did the same prophet then pursue his craft?

CREON

Yes, skilled as now and in no less repute.

OEDIPUS

Did he at that time ever glance at me?

CREON

Not to my knowledge, not when I was by.

OEDIPUS

But was no search and inquisition made?

CREON

Surely full quest was made, but nothing learnt.

OEDIPUS

Why failed the seer to tell his story then?

CREON

I know not, and not knowing hold my tongue.

OEDIPUS

This much thou knowest and canst surely tell.

* * *

CREON

What's mean'st thou? All I know I will declare.

OEDIPUS

But for thy prompting never had the seer

Ascribed to me the death of Laius.

CREON

If so he thou knowest best; but I

Would put thee to the question in my turn.

OEDIPUS

Question and prove me murderer if thou canst.

CREON

Then let me ask thee, didst thou wed my sister?

OEDIPUS

A fact so plain I cannot well deny.

CREON

And as thy consort queen she shares the throne?

OEDIPUS

I grant her freely all her heart desires.

CREON

And with you twain I share the triple rule?

OEDIPUS

Yea, and it is that proves thee a false friend.

CREON

Not so, if thou wouldst reason with thyself,

As I with myself. First, I bid thee think,

Would any mortal choose a troubled reign

Of terrors rather than secure repose,

If the same power were given him?

As for me, I have no natural craving for the name

Of king, preferring to do kingly deeds,

And so thinks every sober-minded man.

Now all my needs are satisfied through thee,

And I have naught to fear; but were I king,

My acts would oft run counter to my will.

How could a title then have charms for me

Above the sweets of boundless influence?

I am not so infatuate as to grasp

The shadow when I hold the substance fast.

Now all men cry me Godspeed! wish me well,

And every suitor seeks to gain my ear,

If he would hope to win a grace from thee.

Why should I leave the better, choose the worse?

That were sheer madness, and I am not mad.

No such ambition ever tempted me,

Nor would I have a share in such intrigue.

And if thou doubt me, first to Delphi go,

There ascertain if my report was true

Of the god's answer; next investigate

If with the seer I plotted or conspired,

And if it prove so, sentence me to death,

Not by thy voice alone, but mine and thine.

But O condemn me not, without appeal,

On bare suspicion. 'Tis not right to adjudge

Bad men at random good, or good men bad.

I would as lief a man should cast away

The thing he counts most precious, his own life,

As spurn a true friend. Thou wilt learn in time

The truth, for time alone reveals the just;

A villain is detected in a day.

CHORUS
To one who walketh warily his words

Commend themselves; swift counsels are not sure.

OEDIPUS

When with swift strides the stealthy plotter stalks

I must be quick too with my counterplot.

To wait his onset passively, for him

Is sure success, for me assured defeat.

CREON

What then's thy will? To banish me the land?

OEDIPUS

I would not have thee banished, no, but dead,

That men may mark the wages envy reaps.

CREON

I see thou wilt not yield, nor credit me.

OEDIPUS

None but a fool would credit such as thou.

CREON

Thou art not wise.

OEDIPUS

Wise for myself at least.

CREON

Why not for me too?

OEDIPUS

Why for such a knave?

* * *

CREON

Suppose thou lackest sense.

OEDIPUS

Yet kings must rule.

CREON

Not if they rule ill.

OEDIPUS

Oh my Thebans, hear him!

CREON

Thy Thebans? am not I a Theban too?

CHORUS

Cease, princes; lo there comes, and none too soon,

Jocasta from the palace.

Who so fit

As peacemaker to reconcile your feud?

[Enter JOCASTA.]

JOCASTA

Misguided princes, why have ye upraised

This wordy wrangle?

Are ye not ashamed,

While the whole land lies stricken, thus to voice

Your private injuries?

Go in, my lord; Go home, my brother, and forebear to make

A public scandal of a petty grief.

CREON
My royal sister, Oedipus, thy lord,

Hath bid me choose (O dread alternative!)

An outlaw's exile or a felon's death.

OEDIPUS
Yes, lady; I have caught him practicing

Against my royal person his vile arts.

CREON
May I ne'er speed but die accursed, if I

In any way am guilty of this charge.

JOCASTA
Believe him, I adjure thee, Oedipus,

First for his solemn oath's sake, then for mine,

And for thine elders' sake who wait on thee.

CHORUS
(Str. 1)
Hearken, King, reflect, we pray thee, be not stubborn but relent.

* * *

OEDIPUS

Say to what should I consent?

CHORUS

Respect a man whose probity and troth

Are known to all and now confirmed by oath.

OEDIPUS

Dost know what grace thou cravest?

CHORUS

Yea, I know.

OEDIPUS

Declare it then and make thy meaning plain.

CHORUS

Brand not a friend whom babbling tongues assail;

Let not suspicion 'gainst his oath prevail.

OEDIPUS

Bethink you that in seeking this ye seek

In very sooth my death or banishment?

CHORUS

No, by the leader of the host divine!

(Str. 2)
Witness, thou Sun, such thought was never mine,

Unblest, unfriended may I perish,

If ever I such wish did cherish!

But O my heart is desolate

Musing on our stricken State,

Doubly fall'n should discord grow

Twixt you twain, to crown our woe.

OEDIPUS
Well, let him go, no matter what it cost me,

Or certain death or shameful banishment,

For your sake I relent, not his; and him,

Where'er he be, my heart shall still abhor.

CREON
Thou art as sullen in thy yielding mood

As in thine anger thou wast truculent.

Such tempers justly plague themselves the most.

OEDIPUS
Leave me in peace and get thee gone.

CREON
I go,

By thee misjudged, but justified by these.

[Exeunt CREON]

CHORUS
(Ant. 1)
Lady, lead indoors thy consort; wherefore longer here delay?

JOCASTA
Tell me first how rose the fray.

CHORUS
Rumors bred unjust suspicious and injustice rankles sore.

JOCASTA
Were both at fault?

CHORUS
Both.

JOCASTA
What was the tale?

CHORUS
Ask me no more. The land is sore distressed;

'Twere better sleeping ills to leave at rest.

OEDIPUS
Strange counsel, friend!

I know thou mean'st me well,

And yet would'st mitigate and blunt my zeal.

CHORUS
(Ant. 2)
King, I say it once again,
Witless were I proved, insane,

If I lightly put away
Thee my country's prop and stay,
Pilot who, in danger sought,
To a quiet haven brought
Our distracted State; and now
Who can guide us right but thou?

JOCASTA

Let me too, I adjure thee, know, O king,

What cause has stirred this unrelenting wrath.

OEDIPUS

I will, for thou art more to me than these.

Lady, the cause is Creon and his plots.

JOCASTA

But what provoked the quarrel? make this clear.

OEDIPUS

He points me out as Laius' murderer.

JOCASTA

Of his own knowledge or upon report?

OEDIPUS

He is too cunning to commit himself,

And makes a mouthpiece of a knavish seer.

JOCASTA

Then thou mayest ease thy conscience on that score.

Listen and I'll convince thee that no man

Hath scot or lot in the prophetic art.

Here is the proof in brief. An oracle

Once came to Laius (I will not say

'Twas from the Delphic god himself, but from

His ministers) declaring he was doomed

To perish by the hand of his own son,

A child that should be born to him by me.

Now Laius--so at least report affirmed--

Was murdered on a day by highwaymen,

No natives, at a spot where three roads meet.

As for the child, it was but three days old,

When Laius, its ankles pierced and pinned

Together, gave it to be cast away

By others on the trackless mountain side.

So then Apollo brought it not to pass

The child should be his father's murderer,

Or the dread terror find accomplishment,

And Laius be slain by his own son.

Such was the prophet's horoscope. O king,

Regard it not.

Whate'er the god deems fit

To search, himself unaided will reveal.

OEDIPUS
What memories, what wild tumult of the soul

Came o'er me, lady, as I heard thee speak!

JOCASTA
What mean'st thou? What has shocked and startled thee?

OEDIPUS
Methought I heard thee say that Laius

Was murdered at the meeting of three roads.

JOCASTA
So ran the story that is current still.

OEDIPUS
Where did this happen? Dost thou know the place?

JOCASTA
Phocis the land is called; the spot is where

Branch roads from Delphi and from Daulis meet.

OEDIPUS
And how long is it since these things befell?

JOCASTA
'Twas but a brief while were thou wast proclaimed

Our country's ruler that the news was brought.

* * *

OEDIPUS

O Zeus, what hast thou willed to do with me!

JOCASTA

What is it, Oedipus, that moves thee so?

OEDIPUS

Ask me not yet; tell me the build and height

Of Laius? Was he still in manhood's prime?

JOCASTA

Tall was he, and his hair was lightly strewn

With silver; and not unlike thee in form.

OEDIPUS

O woe is me! Methinks unwittingly

I laid but now a dread curse on myself.

JOCASTA

What say'st thou? When I look upon thee, my king, I tremble.

OEDIPUS

'Tis a dread presentiment

That in the end the seer will prove not blind.

One further question to resolve my doubt.

JOCASTA

I quail; but ask, and I will answer all.

* * *

OEDIPUS

Had he but few attendants or a train

Of armed retainers with him, like a prince?

JOCASTA

They were but five in all, and one of them

A herald; Laius in a mule-car rode.

OEDIPUS

Alas! 'tis clear as noonday now. But say,

Lady, who carried this report to Thebes?

JOCASTA

A serf, the sole survivor who returned.

OEDIPUS

Haply he is at hand or in the house?

JOCASTA

No, for as soon as he returned and found

Thee reigning in the stead of Laius slain,

He clasped my hand and supplicated me

To send him to the alps and pastures, where

He might be farthest from the sight of Thebes.

And so I sent him. 'Twas an honest slave

And well deserved some better recompense.

* * *

OEDIPUS
Fetch him at once. I fain would see the man.

JOCASTA
He shall be brought; but wherefore summon him?

OEDIPUS
Lady, I fear my tongue has overrun

Discretion; therefore I would question him.

JOCASTA
Well, he shall come, but may not I too claim

To share the burden of thy heart, my king?

OEDIPUS
And thou shalt not be frustrate of thy wish.

Now my imaginings have gone so far.

Who has a higher claim that thou to hear

My tale of dire adventures? Listen then.

My sire was Polybus of Corinth, and

My mother Merope, a Dorian;

And I was held the foremost citizen,

Till a strange thing befell me, strange indeed,

Yet scarce deserving all the heat it stirred.

A roisterer at some banquet, flown with wine,

Shouted "Thou art not true son of thy sire."

It irked me, but I stomached for the nonce

The insult; on the morrow I sought out

My mother and my sire and questioned them.

They were indignant at the random slur

Cast on my parentage and did their best

To comfort me, but still the venomed barb

Rankled, for still the scandal spread and grew.

So privily without their leave I went

To Delphi, and Apollo sent me back

Baulked of the knowledge that I came to seek.

But other grievous things he prophesied,

Woes, lamentations, mourning, portents dire;

To wit I should defile my mother's bed

And raise up seed too loathsome to behold,

And slay the father from whose loins I sprang.

Then, lady,--thou shalt hear the very truth--

As I drew near the triple-branching roads,

A herald met me and a man who sat

In a car drawn by colts--as in thy tale--

The man in front and the old man himself

Threatened to thrust me rudely from the path,

Then jostled by the charioteer in wrath I struck him, and the old man, seeing this,

Watched till I passed and from his car brought down

Full on my head the double-pointed goad.

Yet was I quits with him and more; one stroke

Of my good staff sufficed to fling him clean

Out of the chariot seat and laid him prone.

And so I slew them every one. But if

Betwixt this stranger there was aught in common

With Laius, who more miserable than I,

What mortal could you find more god-abhorred?

Wretch whom no sojourner, no citizen

May harbor or address, whom all are bound

To harry from their homes. And this same curse

Was laid on me, and laid by none but me.

Yea with these hands all gory I pollute

The bed of him I slew. Say, am I vile?

Am I not utterly unclean, a wretch

Doomed to be banished, and in banishment

Forgo the sight of all my dearest ones,

And never tread again my native earth;

Or else to wed my mother and slay my sire,

Polybus, who begat me and upreared?

If one should say, this is the handiwork

Of some inhuman power, who could blame

His judgment? But, ye pure and awful gods,

Forbid, forbid that I should see that day!

May I be blotted out from living men

Ere such a plague spot set on me its brand!

CHORUS
We too, O king, are troubled; but till thou

Hast questioned the survivor, still hope on.

OEDIPUS
My hope is faint, but still enough survives

To bid me bide the coming of this herd.

JOCASTA
Suppose him here, what wouldst thou learn of him?

* * *

OEDIPUS

I'll tell thee, lady; if his tale agrees

With thine, I shall have 'scaped calamity.

JOCASTA

And what of special import did I say?

OEDIPUS

In thy report of what the herdsman said

Laius was slain by robbers; now if he

Still speaks of robbers, not a robber, I

Slew him not; "one" with "many" cannot square.

But if he says one lonely wayfarer,

The last link wanting to my guilt is forged.

JOCASTA

Well, rest assured, his tale ran thus at first,

Nor can he now retract what then he said;

Not I alone but all our townsfolk heard it.

E'en should he vary somewhat in his story,

He cannot make the death of Laius

In any wise jump with the oracle.

For Loxias said expressly he was doomed

To die by my child's hand, but he, poor babe,

He shed no blood, but perished first himself.

So much for divination.

Henceforth I Will look for signs neither to right nor left.

OEDIPUS
Thou reasonest well. Still I would have thee send

And fetch the bondsman hither. See to it.

JOCASTA
That will I straightway. Come, let us within.

I would do nothing that my lord mislikes.

[Exeunt OEDIPUS and JOCASTA]

CHORUS
(Str. 1)
My lot be still to lead

The life of innocence and fly

Irreverence in word or deed,

To follow still those laws ordained on high

Whose birthplace is the bright ethereal sky

No mortal birth they own,

Olympus their progenitor alone:

Ne'er shall they slumber in oblivion cold,

The god in them is strong and grows not old.

(Ant. 1)

Of insolence is bred The tyrant; insolence full blown,

With empty riches surfeited,

Scales the precipitous height and grasps the throne.

Then topples o'er and lies in ruin prone;

No foothold on that dizzy steep.

But O may Heaven the true patriot keep

Who burns with emulous zeal to serve the State.

God is my help and hope, on him I wait.

(Str. 2)
But the proud sinner, or in word or deed,

That will not Justice heed,

Nor reverence the shrine

Of images divine,

Perdition seize his vain imaginings,

If, urged by greed profane,

He grasps at ill-got gain,

And lays an impious hand on holiest things.

Who when such deeds are done

Can hope heaven's bolts to shun?

If sin like this to honor can aspire,

Why dance I still and lead the sacred choir?

(Ant. 2)
No more I'll seek earth's central oracle,

Or Abae's hallowed cell,

Nor to Olympia bring

My votive offering.

If before all God's truth be not bade plain.

O Zeus, reveal thy might,

King, if thou'rt named aright

Omnipotent, all-seeing, as of old;

For Laius is forgot;

His weird, men heed it not;

Apollo is forsook and faith grows cold.

[Enter JOCASTA.]

* * *

JOCASTA

My lords, ye look amazed to see your queen

With wreaths and gifts of incense in her hands.

I had a mind to visit the high shrines,

For Oedipus is overwrought, alarmed

With terrors manifold. He will not use

His past experience, like a man of sense,

To judge the present need, but lends an ear

To any croaker if he augurs ill.

Since then my counsels naught avail, I turn

To thee, our present help in time of trouble,

Apollo, Lord Lycean, and to thee

My prayers and supplications here I bring.

Lighten us, lord, and cleanse us from this curse!

For now we all are cowed like mariners

Who see their helmsman dumbstruck in the storm.

[Enter Corinthian MESSENGER.]

MESSENGER

My masters, tell me where the palace is

Of Oedipus; or better, where's the king.

CHORUS

Here is the palace and he bides within;

This is his queen the mother of his children.

MESSENGER

All happiness attend her and the house,

Blessed is her husband and her marriage-bed.

JOCASTA

My greetings to thee, stranger; thy fair words

Deserve a like response. But tell me why

Thou comest--what thy need or what thy news.

MESSENGER

Good for thy consort and the royal house.

JOCASTA

What may it be? Whose messenger art thou?

MESSENGER

The Isthmian commons have resolved to make

Thy husband king--so 'twas reported there.

JOCASTA

What! is not aged Polybus still king?

* * *

MESSENGER

No, verily; he's dead and in his grave.

JOCASTA

What! is he dead, the sire of Oedipus?

MESSENGER

If I speak falsely, may I die myself.

JOCASTA

Quick, maiden, bear these tidings to my lord.

Ye god-sent oracles, where stand ye now!

This is the man whom Oedipus long shunned,

In dread to prove his murderer; and now

He dies in nature's course, not by his hand.

[Enter OEDIPUS.]

OEDIPUS

My wife, my queen, Jocasta, why hast thou

Summoned me from my palace?

JOCASTA

Hear this man,

And as thou hearest judge what has become

Of all those awe-inspiring oracles.

OEDIPUS

Who is this man, and what his news for me?

JOCASTA

He comes from Corinth and his message this:

Thy father Polybus hath passed away.

OEDIPUS

What? let me have it, stranger, from thy mouth.

MESSENGER

If I must first make plain beyond a doubt

My message, know that Polybus is dead.

OEDIPUS

By treachery, or by sickness visited?

MESSENGER

One touch will send an old man to his rest.

OEDIPUS

So of some malady he died, poor man.

MESSENGER

Yes, having measured the full span of years.

OEDIPUS

Out on it, lady! why should one regard

The Pythian hearth or birds that scream i' the air?

Did they not point at me as doomed to slay

My father? but he's dead and in his grave

And here am I who ne'er unsheathed a sword;

Unless the longing for his absent son

Killed him and so I slew him in a sense.

But, as they stand, the oracles are dead--

Dust, ashes, nothing, dead as Polybus.

JOCASTA
Say, did not I foretell this long ago?

OEDIPUS
Thou didst: but I was misled by my fear.

JOCASTA
Then let I no more weigh upon thy soul.

OEDIPUS
Must I not fear my mother's marriage bed.

JOCASTA
Why should a mortal man, the sport of chance,

With no assured foreknowledge, be afraid?

Best live a careless life from hand to mouth. T

his wedlock with thy mother fear not thou.

How oft it chances that in dreams a man

Has wed his mother!

He who least regards

Such brainsick phantasies lives most at ease.

OEDIPUS

I should have shared in full thy confidence,

Were not my mother living; since she lives

Though half convinced I still must live in dread.

JOCASTA

And yet thy sire's death lights out darkness much.

OEDIPUS

Much, but my fear is touching her who lives.

MESSENGER

Who may this woman be whom thus you fear?

OEDIPUS

Merope, stranger, wife of Polybus.

MESSENGER

And what of her can cause you any fear?

OEDIPUS

A heaven-sent oracle of dread import.

MESSENGER

A mystery, or may a stranger hear it?

OEDIPUS

Aye, 'tis no secret. Loxias once foretold

That I should mate with mine own mother, and shed

With my own hands the blood of my own sire.

Hence Corinth was for many a year to me

A home distant; and I trove abroad,

But missed the sweetest sight, my parents' face.

MESSENGER
Was this the fear that exiled thee from home?

OEDIPUS
Yea, and the dread of slaying my own sire.

MESSENGER
Why, since I came to give thee pleasure, King,

Have I not rid thee of this second fear?

OEDIPUS
Well, thou shalt have due guerdon for thy pains.

MESSENGER
Well, I confess what chiefly made me come

Was hope to profit by thy coming home.

OEDIPUS
Nay, I will ne'er go near my parents more.

MESSENGER
My son, 'tis plain, thou know'st not what thou doest.

OEDIPUS
How so, old man? For heaven's sake tell me all.

MESSENGER
If this is why thou dreadest to return.

OEDIPUS

Yea, lest the god's word be fulfilled in me.

MESSENGER

Lest through thy parents thou shouldst be accursed?

OEDIPUS

This and none other is my constant dread.

MESSENGER

Dost thou not know thy fears are baseless all?

OEDIPUS

How baseless, if I am their very son?

MESSENGER

Since Polybus was naught to thee in blood.

OEDIPUS

What say'st thou? was not Polybus my sire?

MESSENGER

As much thy sire as I am, and no more.

OEDIPUS

My sire no more to me than one who is naught?

MESSENGER

Since I begat thee not, no more did he.

OEDIPUS

What reason had he then to call me son?

MESSENGER

Know that he took thee from my hands, a gift.

* * *

OEDIPUS
Yet, if no child of his, he loved me well.

MESSENGER
A childless man till then, he warmed to thee.

OEDIPUS
A foundling or a purchased slave, this child?

MESSENGER
I found thee in Cithaeron's wooded glens.

OEDIPUS
What led thee to explore those upland glades?

MESSENGER
My business was to tend the mountain flocks.

OEDIPUS
A vagrant shepherd journeying for hire?

MESSENGER
True, but thy savior in that hour, my son.

OEDIPUS
My savior? from what harm? what ailed me then?

MESSENGER
Those ankle joints are evidence enow.

OEDIPUS
Ah, why remind me of that ancient sore?

***

MESSENGER

I loosed the pin that riveted thy feet.

OEDIPUS

Yes, from my cradle that dread brand I bore.

MESSENGER

Whence thou deriv'st the name that still is thine.

OEDIPUS

Who did it? I adjure thee, tell me who

Say, was it father, mother?

MESSENGER

I know not.

The man from whom I had thee may know more.

OEDIPUS

What, did another find me, not thyself?

MESSENGER

Not I; another shepherd gave thee me.

OEDIPUS

Who was he? Would'st thou know again the man?

MESSENGER

He passed indeed for one of Laius' house.

OEDIPUS

The king who ruled the country long ago?

MESSENGER
The same: he was a herdsman of the king.

OEDIPUS
And is he living still for me to see him?

MESSENGER
His fellow-countrymen should best know that.

OEDIPUS
Doth any bystander among you know

The herd he speaks of, or by seeing him

Afield or in the city? answer straight!

The hour hath come to clear this business up.

CHORUS
Methinks he means none other than the hind

Whom thou anon wert fain to see; but that

Our queen Jocasta best of all could tell.

OEDIPUS
Madam, dost know the man we sent to fetch?

Is the same of whom the stranger speaks?

JOCASTA
Who is the man? What matter? Let it be.

'Twere waste of thought to weigh such idle words.

OEDIPUS
No, with such guiding clues I cannot fail

To bring to light the secret of my birth.

JOCASTA
Oh, as thou carest for thy life, give o'er

This quest. Enough the anguish I endure.

OEDIPUS
Be of good cheer; though I be proved the son

Of a bondwoman, aye, through three descents

Triply a slave, thy honor is unsmirched.

JOCASTA
Yet humor me, I pray thee; do not this.

OEDIPUS
I cannot; I must probe this matter home.

JOCASTA
'Tis for thy sake I advise thee for the best.

OEDIPUS
I grow impatient of this best advice.

JOCASTA
Ah mayst thou ne'er discover who thou art!

OEDIPUS
Go, fetch me here the herd, and leave yon woman

To glory in her pride of ancestry.

JOCASTA
O woe is thee, poor wretch!

With that last word I leave thee, henceforth silent evermore.

[Exit JOCASTA]

CHORUS

Why, Oedipus, why stung with passionate grief

Hath the queen thus departed? Much I fear

From this dead calm will burst a storm of woes.

OEDIPUS

Let the storm burst, my fixed resolve still holds,

To learn my lineage, be it ne'er so low.

It may be she with all a woman's pride

Thinks scorn of my base parentage. But I

Who rank myself as Fortune's favorite child,

The giver of good gifts, shall not be shamed.

She is my mother and the changing moons

My brethren, and with them I wax and wane.

Thus sprung why should I fear to trace my birth?

Nothing can make me other than I am.

CHORUS
(Str.)
If my soul prophetic err not, if my wisdom aught avail,

Thee, Cithaeron, I shall hail,

As the nurse and foster-mother of our Oedipus shall greet

Ere tomorrow's full moon rises, and exalt thee as is meet.

Dance and song shall hymn thy praises, lover of our royal race.

Phoebus, may my words find grace!

(Ant.)
Child, who bare thee, nymph or goddess? sure thy sure was more than man

Haply the hill-roamer Pan.

Of did Loxias beget thee, for he haunts the upland wold;

Or Cyllene's lord, or Bacchus, dweller on the hilltops cold?

Did some Heliconian Oread give him thee, a new-born joy?

Nymphs with whom he love to toy?

OEDIPUS
Elders, if I, who never yet before

Have met the man, may make a guess, methinks

I see the herdsman who we long have sought;

His time-worn aspect matches with the years

Of yonder aged messenger; besides I seem to recognize the men who bring him

As servants of my own. But you, perchance,

Having in past days known or seen the herd,

May better by sure knowledge my surmise.

CHORUS
I recognize him; one of Laius' house; A simple hind, but true as any man.

[Enter HERDSMAN.]

OEDIPUS
Corinthian, stranger, I address thee first,

Is this the man thou meanest!

MESSENGER
This is he.

OEDIPUS
And now old man, look up and answer all I ask thee.

Wast thou once of Laius' house?

HERDSMAN
I was, a thrall, not purchased but home-bred.

OEDIPUS
What was thy business? how wast thou employed?

HERDSMAN

The best part of my life I tended sheep.

OEDIPUS

What were the pastures thou didst most frequent?

HERDSMAN

Cithaeron and the neighboring alps.

OEDIPUS

Then there

Thou must have known yon man, at least by fame?

HERDSMAN

Yon man? in what way? what man dost thou mean?

OEDIPUS

The man here, having met him in past times...

HERDSMAN

Off-hand I cannot call him well to mind.

MESSENGER

No wonder, master. But I will revive

His blunted memories. Sure he can recall

What time together both we drove our flocks,

He two, I one, on the Cithaeron range,

For three long summers; I his mate from spring

Till rose Arcturus; then in winter time

I led mine home, he his to Laius' folds.

Did these things happen as I say, or no?

HERDSMAN
'Tis long ago, but all thou say'st is true.

MESSENGER
Well, thou mast then remember giving me

A child to rear as my own foster-son?

HERDSMAN
Why dost thou ask this question? What of that?

MESSENGER
Friend, he that stands before thee was that child.

HERDSMAN
A plague upon thee! Hold thy wanton tongue!

OEDIPUS
Softly, old man, rebuke him not; thy words

Are more deserving chastisement than his.

HERDSMAN
O best of masters, what is my offense?

OEDIPUS
Not answering what he asks about the child.

HERDSMAN
He speaks at random, babbles like a fool.

OEDIPUS
If thou lack'st grace to speak, I'll loose thy tongue.

* * *

HERDSMAN

For mercy's sake abuse not an old man.

OEDIPUS

Arrest the villain, seize and pinion him!

HERDSMAN

Alack, alack!
What have I done? what wouldst thou further learn?

OEDIPUS

Didst give this man the child of whom he asks?

HERDSMAN

I did; and would that I had died that day!

OEDIPUS

And die thou shalt unless thou tell the truth.

HERDSMAN

But, if I tell it, I am doubly lost.

OEDIPUS

The knave methinks will still prevaricate.

HERDSMAN

Nay, I confessed I gave it long ago.

OEDIPUS

Whence came it? was it thine, or given to thee?

HERDSMAN

I had it from another, 'twas not mine.

OEDIPUS

From whom of these our townsmen, and what house?

HERDSMAN

Forbear for God's sake, master, ask no more.

OEDIPUS

If I must question thee again, thou'rt lost.

HERDSMAN

Well then--it was a child of Laius' house.

OEDIPUS

Slave-born or one of Laius' own race?

HERDSMAN

Ah me!
I stand upon the perilous edge of speech.

OEDIPUS

And I of hearing, but I still must hear.

HERDSMAN

Know then the child was by repute his own,

But she within, thy consort best could tell.

OEDIPUS

What! she, she gave it thee?

HERDSMAN

'Tis so, my king.

OEDIPUS

With what intent?

* * *

HERDSMAN
To make away with it.

OEDIPUS
What, she its mother.

HERDSMAN
Fearing a dread weird.

OEDIPUS
What weird?

HERDSMAN
'Twas told that he should slay his sire.

OEDIPUS
What didst thou give it then to this old man?

HERDSMAN
Through pity, master, for the babe. I thought

He'd take it to the country whence he came;

But he preserved it for the worst of woes.

For if thou art in sooth what this man saith,

God pity thee! thou wast to misery born.

OEDIPUS
Ah me! ah me! all brought to pass, all true!

O light, may I behold thee nevermore!

I stand a wretch, in birth, in wedlock cursed,

A parricide, incestuously, triply cursed!

[Exit OEDIPUS]

CHORUS
(Str. 1)
Races of mortal man

Whose life is but a span,

I count ye but the shadow of a shade!

For he who most doth know

Of bliss, hath but the show;

A moment, and the visions pale and fade.

Thy fall, O Oedipus, thy piteous fall

Warns me none born of women blest to call.

(Ant. 1)
For he of marksmen best, O Zeus, outshot the rest,

And won the prize supreme of wealth and power.

By him the vulture maid

Was quelled, her witchery laid;

He rose our savior and the land's strong tower.

We hailed thee king and from that day adored

Of mighty Thebes the universal lord.

(Str. 2)
O heavy hand of fate!
Who now more desolate,

Whose tale more sad than thine, whose lot more dire?

O Oedipus, discrowned head,

Thy cradle was thy marriage bed;

One harborage sufficed for son and sire.

How could the soil thy father eared so long

Endure to bear in silence such a wrong?

(Ant. 2)
All-seeing Time hath caught Guilt, and to justice brought

The son and sire commingled in one bed.

O child of Laius' ill-starred race

Would I had ne'er beheld thy face;

I raise for thee a dirge as o'er the dead.

Yet, sooth to say, through thee I drew new breath,

And now through thee I feel a second death.

[Enter SECOND MESSENGER.]

SECOND MESSENGER

Most grave and reverend senators of Thebes,

What Deeds ye soon must hear, what sights behold

How will ye mourn, if, true-born patriots,

Ye reverence still the race of Labdacus!

Not Ister nor all Phasis' flood, I ween,

Could wash away the blood-stains from this house,

The ills it shrouds or soon will bring to light,

Ills wrought of malice, not unwittingly.

The worst to bear are self-inflicted wounds.

CHORUS

Grievous enough for all our tears and groans

Our past calamities; what canst thou add?

SECOND MESSENGER

My tale is quickly told and quickly heard.

Our sovereign lady queen Jocasta's dead.

CHORUS
Alas, poor queen! how came she by her death?

SECOND MESSENGER
By her own hand. And all the horror of it,

Not having seen, yet cannot comprehend.

Nathless, as far as my poor memory serves,

I will relate the unhappy lady's woe.

When in her frenzy she had passed inside

The vestibule, she hurried straight to win

The bridal-chamber, clutching at her hair

With both her hands, and, once within the room,

She shut the doors behind her with a crash.

"Laius," she cried, and called her husband dead

Long, long ago; her thought was of that child

By him begot, the son by whom the sire

Was murdered and the mother left to breed

With her own seed, a monstrous progeny.

Then she bewailed the marriage bed whereon

Poor wretch, she had conceived a double brood,

Husband by husband, children by her child.

What happened after that I cannot tell,

Nor how the end befell, for with a shriek

Burst on us Oedipus; all eyes were fixed

On Oedipus, as up and down he strode,

Nor could we mark her agony to the end.

For stalking to and fro

"A sword!" he cried,

"Where is the wife, no wife, the teeming womb

That bore a double harvest, me and mine?"

And in his frenzy some supernal power

(No mortal, surely, none of us who watched him)

Guided his footsteps; with a terrible shriek,

As though one beckoned him, he crashed against

The folding doors, and from their staples forced

The wrenched bolts and hurled himself within.

Then we beheld the woman hanging there,

A running noose entwined about her neck.

But when he saw her, with a maddened roar

He loosed the cord; and when her wretched corpse

Lay stretched on earth, what followed--O 'twas dread!

He tore the golden brooches that upheld

Her queenly robes, upraised them high and smote

Full on his eye-balls, uttering words like these:

"No more shall ye behold such sights of woe,

Deeds I have suffered and myself have wrought;

Henceforward quenched in darkness shall ye see

Those ye should ne'er have seen; now blind to those

Whom, when I saw, I vainly yearned to know."

Such was the burden of his moan, whereto,

Not once but oft, he struck with his hand uplift

His eyes, and at each stroke the ensanguined orbs

Bedewed his beard, not oozing drop by drop,

But one black gory downpour, thick as hail.

Such evils, issuing from the double source,

Have whelmed them both, confounding man and wife.

Till now the storied fortune of this house

Was fortunate indeed; but from this day

Woe, lamentation, ruin, death, disgrace,

All ills that can be named, all, all are theirs.

* * *

CHORUS
But hath he still no respite from his pain?

SECOND MESSENGER
He cries, "Unbar the doors and let all Thebes

Behold the slayer of his sire, his mother's--"

That shameful word my lips may not repeat.

He vows to fly self-banished from the land,

Nor stay to bring upon his house the curse

Himself had uttered; but he has no strength

Nor one to guide him, and his torture's more

Than man can suffer, as yourselves will see.

For lo, the palace portals are unbarred,

And soon ye shall behold a sight so sad

That he who must abhorred would pity it.

[Enter OEDIPUS blinded.]

CHORUS
Woeful sight! more woeful none

These sad eyes have looked upon.

Whence this madness? None can tell

Who did cast on thee his spell, prowling all thy life around,

Leaping with a demon bound.

Hapless wretch! how can I brook

On thy misery to look?

Though to gaze on thee I yearn,

Much to question, much to learn,

Horror-struck away I turn.

OEDIPUS
Ah me! ah woe is me!
Ah whither am I borne!
How like a ghost forlorn
My voice flits from me on the air!

On, on the demon goads.

The end, ah where?

CHORUS
An end too dread to tell, too dark to see.

OEDIPUS
(Str. 1)
Dark, dark! The horror of darkness, like a shroud,

Wraps me and bears me on through mist and cloud.

Ah me, ah me!

What spasms athwart me shoot,

What pangs of agonizing memory?

CHORUS
No marvel if in such a plight thou feel'st

The double weight of past and present woes.

OEDIPUS
(Ant. 1)
Ah friend, still loyal, constant still and kind,

Thou carest for the blind.

I know thee near, and though bereft of eyes,

Thy voice I recognize.

CHORUS
O doer of dread deeds, how couldst thou mar

Thy vision thus? What demon goaded thee?

OEDIPUS
(Str. 2)
Apollo, friend, Apollo, he it was

That brought these ills to pass;

But the right hand that dealt the blow

Was mine, none other. How,

How, could I longer see when sight

Brought no delight?

CHORUS
Alas! 'tis as thou sayest.

OEDIPUS
Say, friends, can any look or voice

Or touch of love henceforth my heart rejoice?

Haste, friends, no fond delay,

Take the twice cursed away

Far from all ken,

The man abhorred of gods, accursed of men.

CHORUS
O thy despair well suits thy desperate case.

Would I had never looked upon thy face!

OEDIPUS
(Ant. 2)
My curse on him whoe'er unrived
The waif's fell fetters and my life revived!

He meant me well, yet had he left me there,

He had saved my friends and me a world of care.

CHORUS
I too had wished it so.

OEDIPUS
Then had I never come to shed

My father's blood nor climbed my mother's bed;

The monstrous offspring of a womb defiled,

Co-mate of him who gendered me, and child.

Was ever man before afflicted thus, Like Oedipus.

CHORUS
I cannot say that thou hast counseled well,

For thou wert better dead than living blind.

OEDIPUS
What's done was well done.

Thou canst never shake

My firm belief. A truce to argument.

For, had I sight, I know not with what eyes

I could have met my father in the shades,

Or my poor mother, since against the twain

I sinned, a sin no gallows could atone.

Aye, but, ye say, the sight of children joys

A parent's eyes. What, born as mine were born?

No, such a sight could never bring me joy;

Nor this fair city with its battlements,

Its temples and the statues of its gods,

Sights from which I, now wretchedst of all,

Once ranked the foremost Theban in all Thebes,

By my own sentence am cut off, condemned

By my own proclamation 'gainst the wretch,

The miscreant by heaven itself declared

Unclean--and of the race of Laius.

Thus branded as a felon by myself,

How had I dared to look you in the face?

Nay, had I known a way to choke the springs

Of hearing, I had never shrunk to make

A dungeon of this miserable frame,

Cut off from sight and hearing; for 'tis bliss to bide in regions
sorrow cannot reach.

Why didst thou harbor me, Cithaeron, why

Didst thou not take and slay me? Then I never

Had shown to men the secret of my birth.

O Polybus, O Corinth, O my home,

Home of my ancestors (so wast thou called)

How fair a nursling then I seemed, how foul

The canker that lay festering in the bud!

Now is the blight revealed of root and fruit.

Ye triple high-roads, and thou hidden glen,

Coppice, and pass where meet the three-branched ways,

Ye drank my blood, the life-blood these hands spilt,

My father's; do ye call to mind perchance

Those deeds of mine ye witnessed and the work I wrought thereafter when I came to Thebes?

O fatal wedlock, thou didst give me birth,

And, having borne me, sowed again my seed,

Mingling the blood of fathers, brothers, children,

Brides, wives and mothers, an incestuous brood,

All horrors that are wrought beneath the sun,

Horrors so foul to name them were unmeet.

O, I adjure you, hide me anywhere

Far from this land, or slay me straight, or cast me

Down to the depths of ocean out of sight.

Come hither, deign to touch an abject wretch;

Draw near and fear not; I myself must bear

The load of guilt that none but I can share.

* * *

[Enter CREON.]

CREON

Lo, here is Creon, the one man to grant

Thy prayer by action or advice, for he

Is left the State's sole guardian in thy stead.

OEDIPUS

Ah me! what words to accost him can I find?

What cause has he to trust me?

In the past I have bee proved his rancorous enemy.

CREON

Not in derision, Oedipus, I come
Nor to upbraid thee with thy past misdeeds.

(To BYSTANDERS)
But shame upon you! if ye feel no sense

Of human decencies, at least revere

The Sun whose light beholds and nurtures all.

Leave not thus nakedly for all to gaze at

A horror neither earth nor rain from heaven

Nor light will suffer. Lead him straight within,

For it is seemly that a kinsman's woes

Be heard by kin and seen by kin alone.

OEDIPUS

O listen, since thy presence comes to me

A shock of glad surprise--so noble thou,

And I so vile--O grant me one small boon.

I ask it not on my behalf, but thine.

CREON

And what the favor thou wouldst crave of me?

OEDIPUS

Forth from thy borders thrust me with all speed;

Set me within some vasty desert where

No mortal voice shall greet me any more.

CREON

This had I done already, but I deemed

It first behooved me to consult the god.

OEDIPUS

His will was set forth fully--to destroy

The parricide, the scoundrel; and I am he.

CREON

Yea, so he spake, but in our present plight

'Twere better to consult the god anew.

OEDIPUS

Dare ye inquire concerning such a wretch?

* * *

CREON
Yea, for thyself wouldst credit now his word.

OEDIPUS
Aye, and on thee in all humility
I lay this charge: let her who lies within

Receive such burial as thou shalt ordain;

Such rites 'tis thine, as brother, to perform.

But for myself, O never let my Thebes,

The city of my sires, be doomed to bear

The burden of my presence while I live.

No, let me be a dweller on the hills,

On yonder mount Cithaeron, famed as mine,

My tomb predestined for me by my sire

And mother, while they lived, that I may die

Slain as they sought to slay me, when alive.

This much I know full surely, nor disease

Shall end my days, nor any common chance;

For I had ne'er been snatched from death, unless I was
predestined to some awful doom.

So be it. I reck not how

Fate deals with me

But my unhappy children--for my sons

Be not concerned, O Creon, they are men,

And for themselves, where'er they be, can fend.

But for my daughters twain, poor innocent maids,

Who ever sat beside me at the board

Sharing my viands, drinking of my cup,

For them, I pray thee, care, and, if thou willst,

O might I feel their touch and make my moan.

Hear me, O prince, my noble-hearted prince!

Could I but blindly touch them with my hands

I'd think they still were mine, as when I saw.

[ANTIGONE and ISMENE are led in.]

What say I? can it be my pretty ones

Whose sobs I hear? Has Creon pitied me

And sent me my two darlings? Can this be?

CREON
'Tis true; 'twas I procured thee this delight,

Knowing the joy they were to thee of old.

* * *

OEDIPUS

God speed thee! and as meed for bringing them

May Providence deal with thee kindlier

Than it has dealt with me! O children mine,

Where are ye? Let me clasp you with these hands,

A brother's hands, a father's; hands that made

Lack-luster sockets of his once bright eyes;

Hands of a man who blindly, recklessly,

Became your sire by her from whom he sprang.

Though I cannot behold you, I must weep

In thinking of the evil days to come,

The slights and wrongs that men will put upon you.

Where'er ye go to feast or festival,

No merrymaking will it prove for you,

But oft abashed in tears ye will return.

And when ye come to marriageable years,

Where's the bold wooers who will jeopardize

To take unto himself such disrepute

As to my children's children still must cling,

For what of infamy is lacking here?

"Their father slew his father, sowed the seed

Where he himself was gendered, and begat

These maidens at the source wherefrom he sprang."

Such are the gibes that men will cast at you.

Who then will wed you? None, I ween, but ye

Must pine, poor maids, in single barrenness.

O Prince, Menoeceus' son, to thee, I turn,

With the it rests to father them, for we

Their natural parents, both of us, are lost.

O leave them not to wander poor, unwed,

Thy kin, nor let them share my low estate.

O pity them so young, and but for thee

All destitute. Thy hand upon it, Prince.

To you, my children I had much to say,

Were ye but ripe to hear. Let this suffice:

Pray ye may find some home and live content,

And may your lot prove happier than your sire's.

CREON
Thou hast had enough of weeping; pass within.

* * *

OEDIPUS

I must obey,

Though 'tis grievous.

CREON

Weep not, everything must have its day.

OEDIPUS

Well I go, but on conditions.

CREON

What thy terms for going, say.

OEDIPUS

Send me from the land an exile.

CREON

Ask this of the gods, not me.

OEDIPUS

But I am the gods' abhorrence.

CREON

Then they soon will grant thy plea.

OEDIPUS

Lead me hence, then, I am willing.

CREON

Come, but let thy children go.

OEDIPUS

Rob me not of these my children!

* * *

CREON

Crave not mastery in all,

For the mastery that raised thee was thy bane and wrought thy fall.

CHORUS

Look ye, countrymen and Thebans, this is Oedipus the great,

He who knew the Sphinx's riddle and was mightiest in our state.

Who of all our townsmen gazed not on his fame with envious eyes?

Now, in what a sea of troubles sunk and overwhelmed he lies!

Therefore wait to see life's ending ere thou count one mortal blest;

Wait till free from pain and sorrow he has gained his final rest.

ALL ANIMALS GO TO HEAVEN

GEORGE MACDONALD

Available on Amazon